Published by Ladybird Books Ltd
27 Wrights Lane London W8 5TZ
A Penguin Company

LADYBIRD and the device of a Ladybird are trademarks of Ladybird Books Ltd

Disney's
THE
LION KING II
SIMBA'S · PRIDE

Ladybird

The news swept like the wind across the Pride Lands. The animals gathered quickly at the foot of Pride Rock.

High on the ridge stood Simba the Lion King, Nala the Queen, Timon, Pumbaa and Rafiki.

Everyone watched as Rafiki gently lifted a tiny lion cub towards the skies.

"It's a girl! Welcome, Princess Kiara!" he cried.

The two cubs wanted to play together, but Simba and Zira arrived. They glared angrily at each other. It was time for Kovu and Kiara to say goodbye.

Simba warned Kiara to be more careful. "You're going to be queen one day," he told her. "It's part of who you are. We are all one in the Circle of Life."

Kovu was in trouble too. Zira told him to keep away from Kiara. "I'm sorry," said Kovu. "I thought we could be friends."

"Friends?" hissed Zira. But then she had an idea. If Kovu were to be accepted into the pride, then he would have a better chance to destroy Simba.

Seasons passed and Kovu grew into a strong young lion, ready to carry out his mother's evil plans.

And Kiara, now a beautiful lioness, was about to set out on her first hunt alone. "Daddy, you must promise to let me do this on my own," she told Simba. But the Lion King couldn't keep his promise. Secretly, he asked Timon and Pumbaa to go after her.

Kiara was furious when she found them. She raced away towards the grasslands.

But the princess didn't know that Zira's spies were following her. She was running straight into the Outlanders' trap. "Let's light the fires!" laughed Nuka and Vitani.

When Kiara noticed the flames around her, it was too late to escape. But Kovu appeared and bravely dragged the princess away to safety.

Kiara woke up suddenly and leapt to her feet. At first she didn't know the lion in front of her, but then she recognised him.

"Kovu?" she asked.

Simba, Nala and Rafiki arrived. They had seen the fires from Pride Rock and had run to the rescue.

They were glad that Kiara was safe. But they were not pleased to see Kovu, even though he had saved her life.

Kovu slowly approached Simba. "I humbly ask to join your pride," he said. So Simba decided to give the young Outlander a chance. But the Lion King would not let Kovu inside their cave at Pride Rock.

The next morning Kiara asked Kovu to teach her how to hunt. "Relax," said Kovu. "Feel the earth under your paws."

He led her through the long grass and over a hill towards a flock of birds. There they startled Timon and Pumbaa who were searching for bugs.

Kiara and the others raced down the hill, scattering the birds. But they ran straight into a herd of rhinos.

Simba declared peace across the Pride Lands. And a few days later, the whole pride gathered in a circle on the rocks. Kiara and Kovu came in last to complete the ring, and Rafiki gave them his blessing.

The Circle of Life was complete again and the pride could live happily together once more.